SOMETHING REAL

M.CLARKE

Books by Mary Ting

Vesuvian Books (Publisher)

ISAN - International Sensory Assassin Network
Helix (Book 2 of ISAN)
GENES (Book 3 of ISAN)
CODE (Book 4 of ISAN)
AVA (Book 5 of ISAN)

Jaclyn and the Beanstalk

ROSEWIND Books (Publisher)

When the Wind Chimes
The Seashell of 'Ohana

Romance
Always Be My Baby

Fantasy
Once Upon A Legend

The Crossroads Saga
Crossroads
Between
Beyond
Eternity
Halo City (Novella)

Descendant Prophecies Series
From Gods
From Deities

From Origins
From Titans

Secret Knights Series
The Angel Knights (Novella)
The Chosen Knights
The Blessed Knights
The Sacred Knights
Snow Queen

Watcher Series
Book of Watchers
Book of Enchantresses

Books by M. Clarke (Pen Name)
https://amzn.to/3TgpJDM

Something Great Series
Something Real (Novella)
Something Great
Something Wonderful
Something Forever
Something Amazing
Something Precious
Twas The Knight Before Christmas (Novella)

Knight Fashion Series
Sexiest Man Alive
Sexiest Couple Alive
Sexiest Dad Alive

My Clarity Series
My Clarity

My Serenity

Behind The Door Written with Alexandrea Weis

READ Samples at the end of the book:

Something Great

When the Wind Chimes

Once Upon A Legend

Chapter 1
Maxwell

I walked into my office and sat on the leather chair. Finally, I had earned my father's respect and the CEO position at his business — Knight Fashion.

My father built this company from the ground up. All the sweat, dedication, sleepless nights, and time away from home had paid off. Now he was passing the baton to me.

Light footsteps padded. "Mr. Knight."

I spun toward the voice and smiled. "Good morning, Mandy."

Mandy had been promoted as my personal assistant as of that day.

"Mr. Knight." She gave me a curt nod. "Can I get you anything? Coffee?" Her cheeks flushed a bright pink as she smoothed a strand of dark hair behind her ear.

I knew some heads of departments who demanded coffee be at their desk at a specific time, but that wasn't my style. Mandy was not my errand girl.

"Thank you for asking, but that's not part of your job description."

"Oh." Her chestnut eyes widened, and she rewarded me with a bright smile. "If you need me—"

"I'll give you a ring." I weaved around the desk and shoved my hands in my front pockets. "Today is our first day. Take it easy. Get familiar with everything."

After Mandy left and closed the door, I headed to the mesmerizing view of Los Angeles. The window practically took up the back wall.

I had so many things to do, but I wanted to stand here, soak up the sun, and be grateful for everything in my life. I glanced to the left and right and far off to the horizon, my spectacular twenty-eighth-floor view. Although I'd seen that view often in my dad's office, it felt different from my own.

I flinched when my cell buzzed on the desk. My mother's name displayed on it when I picked it up. She likely wanted to wish me well on my first day.

"Good morning, Mom." I leaned on the edge of my desk as I continued to look out the window.

"Hello, sweetheart. You sound so happy this morning. You excited about your new position?"

I was in my late twenties, but I felt like a little boy when she called me *sweetheart*. "Yes. But it doesn't seem all that new."

"You've been shadowing your father for a while, and now I can't believe the time has come for you to run the company. You're going to be great. As for your father, it will take some time for him to get used to the idea he's retired. Did you know he's at work?"

"What?" I hiked an eyebrow. "Then why did he promote me?" I didn't mean to raise my voice.

"You know your dad. He can't stay away. He's probably taking care of loose ends. Don't tell him I told you. Just pretend you don't know."

It would have been easier if she hadn't told me in the first place.

"Sure. I can do that. Besides, I'll be in meetings all day. I doubt I'll run into him."

Mom swallowed. She must be drinking coffee. "Have you seen Matthew?" A weary tone replaced her happy one.

I scrubbed the back of my head. "No. Not yet. I didn't know he was in town."

"He came yesterday. I was hoping he would come for dinner. We had a long talk last night. I wish—"

"Mom." I ran a hand down my face. "He's a big boy. He just needs time to find himself again."

Mom's heavy, concerned sigh echoed in my ear. "It's my fault. I babied him. I suppose he's still young. And I understand about what happened to Tessa, but your father at twenty-one, he had dreams and—"

"We were both spoiled. What can I say?"

"You're right. He'll come around when he's ready. He promised to come by at dinner. I hope he will. Will you come, too?"

"Hold on." I put her on speaker and scrolled to my calendar on my phone. "I'll be over by seven. Sound good?"

She released a long breath. "I can't wait to have both of my boys under the same roof. It's been so long. See you then."

I sat on my leather seat and turned on the computer. After going through a long list of emails, I checked the time. Time to head to the meeting.

Chapter 2
Maxwell

Employees greeted me as I sauntered down the hallway. When I opened the door to the meeting room, everyone was already seated. I glanced at the clock on the wall. I admired their punctuality. Or they wanted to impress the new boss.

I took a tablet out of my briefcase and set it down. My pulse kicked up and I fought the urge to loosen my tie. All eyes settled on me, waiting. I had attended the monthly meetings with department heads countless times, so why did my stomach tumble with nerves?

Piece of cake, Max. Don't be a wuss. Take charge.

I cleared my throat. "Let's begin." I flashed a glance at Mandy, letting her know she could start taking minutes. I unlocked my tablet and opened the agenda. "Before I begin the meeting, I just want to express my gratitude and thank you for all the support you have given my father, and now I hope you'll give to me. It is my honor to work with you all. I still have a lot to learn, but I promise you, I'll be working just as hard, if not harder than my father."

Applause filled the room.

I smiled and met each person's eyes in turn. "Thank you. Let's continue. Sales are doing well. Even going ahead with the online magazine, we've not seen a dip in US, but in Asia we have."

"Having the option to go paperless was an excellent idea," said Victor, the director of formatting.

"Thank you." I dipped my head into a curt nod.

"I have a new global report, Mr. Knight." Carrie from Finance lifted a folder. "This report indicates we're taking a hit in Asia by ten percent."

"I'm aware. I plan to take a trip end of this week. Don't worry, I've got it handled."

"I'm sure you do." Carrie's smile was infectious.

If I wasn't mistaken, her voice hinted a little flirtation.

"A dinner and some sweet-talking won't hurt." I chuckled.

Laughter filled the room.

"Don't forget to hire strippers." Carrie's face turned pink when the room went silent. "Oh my God. I was just joking." Her face flushed brighter.

Chuckles returned.

Carrie's shoulders eased and she flashed a glance my way. Her innocence was quite charming. I hadn't noticed it before.

After I dismissed the meeting, I leaned back in my chair and checked my agenda. I grabbed my briefcase and stepped out. My phone buzzed. I pulled it out from inside my pocket when something—no, some*one*—collided into me. As I stumbled backward, I caught my elbow on the doorway.

"I'm so sorry." The sultry voice told me the person was a female.

Our gazes locked.

I stared into warm, sky-blue eyes, the prettiest I'd ever seen. Her blonde hair cascaded over half her face, but I knew a good-looking woman when I saw one. And she was a goddess.

She stood straight, the top of her head level with my chin. Slowly, her lips curled into a smile brighter than the sunrise, and the gleam in her eyes told me she liked what she saw.

"Apology accepted." I nodded politely and tried not to lower my eyes down her full length.

Don't look. Don't look. It's not professional to look.

Too late. My mind told my eyes to do one thing, but the man in me couldn't help himself. She wore a tight black pencil skirt, and a white sweater hugged the curves of her breasts. My mind wandered to a place it shouldn't.

Stop it. Be professional. But she has no idea I stripped her naked in my mind.

She smiled again, showing me all her pearly, polished teeth, and crouched to pick up something. When she rose, her head stopped right in front of my jewels, long enough to send a hot, tingling sensation down to my toes. Then she met my eyes again as she closed the gap between us.

Wicked witch. She did that on purpose. But oh, how I enjoyed this daring, dangerous encounter.

"Here." She handed me my cell phone. "You dropped this."

I froze for a second, registering her words. "I believe I have. Thank you for picking it up. That was kind of you."

I barely knew what I'd said. Wanting to keep her there with me a bit longer, I babbled nonsense.

"Anyway, my name is Crystal. I was recently hired in the Customer Relations Department as director. I believe we'll be flying together to South Korea."

I swallowed. "I wasn't aware I had a flying partner."

She pushed a lock of hair behind her ear and shifted in her high heels. "I was just informed through email. You were cc'd as well."

I scrunched my face in confusion. "Who sent the email?"

"Mr. Knight."

I gave her a sidelong glance. "You must be mistaken. I'm Mr. Knight."

Crystal leaned closer. Her sweet, flowery perfume floated around me, carrying me away into a dreamland of lust and desire.

"I know who you are, but isn't your father Mr. Knight as well?"

I felt like an idiot. Father wouldn't dare assign me a companion without asking, would he? Yeah, right. He would.

"My father retired. He doesn't get to make the call." My voice stayed tame, but anger made my heart pound faster.

"Oh." She created distance between us. "Then I'm sorry to have brought it up. Maybe you should go speak to him. However, I would love to accompany you on your business trip. You're going to need someone like me as your right hand. Our competitors are aggressive and I know how to do my job to get the deal done. And right now, with Asia slowly sinking away from Knight Fashion, you need all the players in your court. Thank you for your time, Mr. Knight. Think about it." With that, she winked and sauntered away.

I stood there like a horny schoolboy and watched her hips sway, the tightness in her ass making me drool.

Somehow this woman I hardly knew melted me into a puddle.

Chapter 3
Crystal

Maxwell Knight—a man of honor, dignity, not to mention good-looking and quite the great catch—would be mine. He didn't know I existed, but he would after today.

I had called Mandy earlier to get an appointment with Maxwell, but his schedule was jam-packed. She did ask me if it was urgent and said she would squeeze me in, but my meeting with him was not a top priority.

So I had to improvise.

I took a chance and waited by the meeting room. It seemed stalkerish of me, but I had to meet him today.

Employees rushed out. Being recently hired, I recognized only a few of them.

No Maxwell.

Mandy had told me the floor and conference room number. Could she have given me the wrong information? After all, she had only been promoted today.

Lucky girl. I would love to be Maxwell's assistant.

Just as I was about to leave, he came out. I didn't mean to bump into him, but I had dashed toward him without thinking. But colliding into him couldn't have worked any better.

"I'm so sorry." I used my most sultry voice.

Our eyes locked when he recovered his balance. I had seen him on magazines, seen him from a distance, but in person ... his photo didn't do him justice.

Over six feet of him towered over me. His broad shoulders showed both his strength and that he was someone who took care of himself. The dark gray suit highlighted his toned body, and he looked debonair and delicious.

I beamed an approving smile, taking all of him in. He was my candy, and mentally I was licking him all over.

"Apology accepted." He nodded politely.

When his gaze roamed my body, I swear I felt naked. *Take me now.* I would've stripped for him right then and there. And my thoughts wandered to a place it shouldn't.

I reached down to pick up his cell. He didn't seem aware that he'd dropped it. When I rose, I stopped right in front of his family jewels and imagined licking and sucking him. I met his eyes again, closing the gap between us.

"Here." I handed him his cell phone. "You dropped this."

He blinked as if coming out of a stupor. "I believe I have. Thank you for picking it up. That was kind of you."

Maxwell seemed flustered. Had I made him nervous? I snickered under my breath. After I convinced him he needed me for the business trip to South Korea, I sauntered away.

I felt the weight of Maxwell's eyes on me. Hopefully he was staring at my ass, thinking dirty thoughts of us. The same way my mind ran wild with us in bed. *Maxwell Knight, I can't wait to be under the covers with you.*

Chapter 4
Maxwell

"Max." My father gave me a hug and smiled.

Mother embraced me and patted my face. Her infectious smile and joy made me smile, too. I kissed my mother's cheek and passed the foyer, looking for my little brother I'd missed so much. My brother greeted me with a hug when I rounded the corner of the hall.

"Hello, Matt." I tightened my hold on him and let go.

As soon as I passed the kitchen, the aroma of pot roast hit me. I hadn't had much to eat for lunch, and my growling stomach reminded me.

I gave polite nods to the cooks, grabbed a beer out of the fridge, popped the cap open, and settled on the sofa. Matthew dropped next to me.

"Congrats on your new position, boss." Matthew raised his bottle at me.

I tapped it with mine. "Thank you. And don't call me boss."

Matthew leaned back lazily and put his feet on the table. "Well, if I work there, you'll be my boss. So I'm going to call you boss, boss." He smirked.

I raised an eyebrow, reining in the elation coursing through me. "You're going to work with me?"

Matthew gulped a long one. "Yes, I am, but not tomorrow, or in a week. I need another month, I think. I'm getting tired of traveling. I need to settle down. Right next to you, big bro, so I can bug the shit out of you." He chuckled.

"Just don't live across from or beside me. Maybe the next city. Put some miles between us." I lightly punched his arm.

I didn't mean it, of course. Having Matthew in the same city would be enough, but having him even closer would make my day. Family was everything to me, and after Matthew had been gone for so long, I was happy he decided to return to put down roots.

Matthew took another drink and rested an elbow on the sofa cushion. "No matter the miles between us, you know I'll be in your face."

"I wouldn't have it any other way." I grinned. "So, how are things? Have you seen Tess's family?"

The love of Matthew's life had died after a devastating car accident. A drunk driver had hit her car on a rainy day. Tess's family had eventually decided to take her off life support, and Matthew lost himself that day.

I had been there for him, and he did stay with me for a bit. Then he decided to travel by himself for a year. Sometimes he met his friends in Europe, and sometimes he visited other countries by himself.

I never wanted to know what it was like to lose someone you love. Our family had been patient with him. He needed time to heal, time to process and find the meaning of life himself without being told what to do.

"No, I haven't seen them." Matthew shook his head, his expression turned somber. "Can we talk about something else? So anyone special in your life?"

Crystal's face flashed in my mind and my body warmed. "No one special, but maybe I met one today."

Matthew sat up tall and twisted his body to face me. "No, shit. At work? You have to be careful with the ladies there. They're vultures." He snorted. "If things don't work out … well, you know what will happen. And you need to watch out for the gold diggers. They know how much you're worth."

I sighed and ran a hand through my hair. "I know."

"Is she the always-and-forever type?"

Matthew and I had this saying … Don't get attached to a woman unless she's the always-and-forever type.

"I don't know. We haven't gone out on a date yet." I twirled my bottle, watching the liquid swirl. "She's joining me on my business trip to South Korea in two days. I suppose I'll get to know her then."

Matthew hiked up his brow. "Business trip? I see. Don't rush things."

"Who says anything is going to happen?"

"Uh-huh. I know you."

We stopped our conversation when Mom and Dad entered.

"It's so nice to see both of you in the same room." Mom sat next to Matthew, looking nostalgic. "Every time I look at you two, I see my little boys."

Dad squeezed my shoulder, sitting next to me. "I can't believe Max is taking over the company."

"Speaking of which." I twisted at the waist to face my dad. "Did you by any chance set up my itinerary with someone named Crystal? She's the new head of Customer Relations."

Dad peered up to the ceiling and then back at me. "I might have suggested at one of the meetings before today that the customer relations person should go with you, so she could get to know the clients as well. Nothing beats a face-to-face relationship. I've told you that many times. Your job requires travel, as you know I have done. Sometimes, you can't be in two places at once. So it's a good idea for you to have someone as your backup. In the meantime, it's a good idea for Crystal to go with you. It would be a better idea for Matt to go with you, but until he's ready to settle into Knight Fashion, we'll have to train someone else."

Fair enough.

"Well, you boys must be starving. Dinner's ready." Mom led us into the dining room.

Chapter 5
Maxwell

"Good afternoon, Mr. Knight. I was instructed to be here by 11:30 a.m."

I almost dropped my mug of coffee in my private lounge at the airport. "Hello Crystal. You can call me Max."

Crystal leaned against the door. Her long legs looked tanner in the morning sunlight peering through. She wore a tight skirt that stopped above the knee and a button-up white blouse, dipping a bit low. The soft breeze tousled her blonde hair around her face, and I just stood there staring as I sipped my coffee.

Shit. Where were my manners?

"Would you like some coffee?" I took a mug out from the cabinet and placed it under the coffeemaker.

She approached closer. The scent of her flowery perfume put me in a dream world, surrounded by flowers and a naked Crystal.

Stop that.

"You make your own coffee?" She smiled, leaning one hip against the counter while she slowly pushed back her hair with one hand and exposed her neck.

Smooth. Flawless. How I would love to suck that part of her skin.

"Yes. Why wouldn't I?" I took a sip, catching her eyes over the rim of my mug.

She gave me a coy smile, her long eyelashes slightly fluttering like wings on a butterfly. "I think it's sexy when someone high up on the ladder does things for himself instead of relying on a secretary."

The room suddenly felt too small and too hot.

"I have no coffee maker who waits for me at the airport. And I hired Mandy as an executive assistant. She isn't my errand girl. I'm sure she didn't apply for the position to make coffee and pick up dry cleaning."

Crystal took out the mug when the light blinked. She took a sip and then slid her tongue along the rim while she locked eyes with me.

I imagined her tongue licking my dick and then those lips around it, sucking it hard until ... Fuck. *Get your mind out of the gutter.*

"Anyway, shouldn't we get going?" She looked at her Rolex watch.

I blinked out of my daze. "After you."

I watched that fine ass shake to my private plane, ready for takeoff.

Chapter 6
Crystal

I really like Max. Not only for his good looks but for his charisma. From office and tabloid gossip, I could tell he wasn't the type to tell his woman what to do, but instead would inspire her to reach her goals. He knew how to treat a woman. But was he good in bed?

I felt Max's eyes on me all the way up the stairs to the Knights' private plane. I made sure to sway my hips a bit more for him as I tried not to fall or make a fool of myself.

The inside of the plane was more luxurious than I had imagined. Fine-grained leather seats, polished wood compartments, and granite counters for the bar. It was like a mini, fancy hotel room.

"It's a good thing I asked to fly with you." I sat across from him and clasped my seat belt.

"Did you now?" A corner of his lips twitched.

"You have such a beautiful plane. It would be terrible if you didn't share." I crossed my legs so my heel slid close between his knees.

Max stole a glance at my legs, swallowed, and met my eyes. "I don't share what's mine with just anyone, Crystal. You probably already know that about me."

The seriousness of his tone and the way he said my name sent an erotic sensation down to my toes. I leaned back, rubbing my legs, feeling way too hot.

The captain peered through the crack of the door. "Ready for takeoff, Mr. Knight, Ms. Blackwell?"

"Yes, we are, Peter." Max spread his legs farther, his strong hands on his thighs.

"Great." Peter looked behind him and then back to us. "After we take off, Harry will serve you drinks. And when you're ready, your lunch will be served. We have baked salmon, chicken chopped salad, and rice pilaf. Buckle up." He smiled and then closed the door.

Max's eyes roamed my body, though he tried not to show it. I could only guess what he was thinking at that moment. Instead of thinking about what he wanted to do to me, he should put his dirty thoughts into action.

Silence fell between us as the plane lifted off. I looked out the window, as Max looked to be deep in thought. When the plane leveled, he spoke again.

"The chair reclines into a bed if you're in the mood to take a nap. Also, you're welcome to take a shower. You'll find amenities such as a toothbrush, shampoo, bathrobe. Whatever you need."

I dropped my jaw. "You have a shower?"

He snorted. "Yes, and I get that same expression every time I say it."

"Really? How many clients, or perhaps women, have been on the plane with you?"

Max furrowed his brow and crossed one ankle over the other. "That's not an appropriate question, Ms. Blackwell."

I curved my lips wickedly. "I'm sorry. And here I'd thought we were getting to know each other better."

A corner of his mouth lifted. "Very well. Since we're not at the office, ask away. I'll be honest with you."

Max wasn't a stupid man. He knew when a woman flirted. He probably already guessed I would spread my legs for him.

"Have you ever fucked on your plane?"

I thought he would fire me right then and there when he kept silent, but then the corners of his eyes crinkled.

"I've never been asked that question before. I have to say, you're very bold. I could fire you for misconduct or, better yet, sexual harassment."

"You wouldn't dare, Mr. Knight, for I could do similar. But I won't. I really like you. You're the kind of man I want to snatch up and never let go. You're attractive, honest, highly respected by the community and your peers. Everybody in the fashion industry knows who you are. You have no idea of your worth."

His cheeks flushed.

Max placed an elbow on the armrest, his fist under his chin. He surveyed me again without a word.

"No," he said finally.

"Excuse me?" I straightened in my seat.

So did Max, looking more serious. "You asked me if I've ever fucked on my plane. The answer is no."

"Really?" I angled my eyebrows, debating whether to accept his answer. "I don't believe you."

He chuckled. "I wouldn't lie about that. I would want to brag, don't you think?"

"True." I tapped my lips, thinking. I had come too far to back down. "Then perhaps I can be your first."

He shifted in his seat.

I unbuckled and rose. Fixing my eyes to his, I slowly opened my blouse, one button at a time. Then I undid my strapless bra and threw it at him. I pushed my blouse back just enough to show him my breasts. His eyes widened and his gaze flicked toward the cockpit while he clutched my bra.

I unclasped my skirt and dropped it, leaving me completely naked except for my G-string. Since Max hadn't moved, I massaged my breasts as I threw my head back. When he hadn't stopped me, I knew I had him.

Max tensed his thighs, his chest rising and falling as fast as mine. He unbuckled his seat belt, got down on his knees, and planted his mouth on that perfect spot above my belly button while his hands grasped my ass.

I moaned as pleasurable, electric sensations wove through every fiber of my being. Then he trailed his tongue higher and higher until it traced a ring around one nipple. Then he moved to the next.

Oh. My. God.

I trembled when Max sucked harder. My insides begged for more.

"Max." I pulled him up and crushed my lips to his. My hands roamed over his chest, feeling the ridges and valleys of this perfect man.

"Crystal." He pulled back slightly. "Sorry, but I have to do this. You're temporarily fired."

When he lifted me up, I anchored my legs around his hips and kissed him fiercely. He tasted like honey and coffee. His heat and skill met my expectations, and more. I had dreamt of this moment, of being in his arms. He wanted me, and I wanted him. This could be the start of something special.

"You can be my first." He took me to the restroom and locked the door.

Plenty of room. A gorgeous bathroom indeed. Max placed me down on the beige granite counter and …

"Holy shit," I gasped. He licked and flicked his tongue over my clit.

"Max." I groaned and gripped his hair with my hands.

"You taste so good. You're made of sugar."

"Then taste all of me," I breathed, as air squeezed out of me too fast.

And he did.

Max kissed his way up my middle and gently fondled my breast as he nipped and sucked my nipples.

More. I wanted more.

"Harder," I panted.

He inserted his finger inside me, gently moving in and out.

I wanted to combust. Desire exploded within me and pooled in every nerve ending of my body. As he continued, I yanked loose his tie and stripped off his pants and shirt until he only wore his boxers.

I wanted him butt naked and exposed. I wanted all of him.

"Take it off," I growled, stroking the length of his cock outside the fabric.

He did, and then yanked my G-string to the side and entered me.

"Crystal. You feel so amazing." He pumped once, twice, three times, and then he pulled out.

I tugged him closer. "What are you doing? Don't tease me anymore. I want you."

Max raked a hand over his face, his face flushing. "I don't have a condom."

"No need to worry. I'm on the pill. Now fuck me." I spread my legs wider, pushing my knees apart.

Max rewarded me with a sexy grin and thrust inside me again, and again, rocking faster and faster, until I plunged over the edge.

My chest heaved as his hot breath brushed my face and then my mouth. He stopped and lifted me off the counter and twisted me to face the door, with the mirror beside us. I planted my hands on the metal and welcomed the cool surface.

"I'm going to come on your back, and afterward we're going to take a shower together. And as I wash you off, I'm going to take you again."

"I've never been so happy to be fired." I winked at him in the mirror.

I watched our bodies grinding, molding, moving to our own rhythm. There was something hot and sensual about watching Max's dick move in and out of me. As he worked my nipples, he fucked the hell out of me.

Finally, Max squirted all over my back as if marking his territory. He was a wild, untamed animal, and I had unleashed him.

In the shower, he washed me as carefully as if I were made of glass. Then he fucked me raw to my bones.

Chapter 7
Maxwell

We landed in South Korea late afternoon. The traffic was as horrific as in Los Angeles. I had been to this beautiful country before, but today it felt different, as if I were visiting for the first time.

Perhaps going as the new CEO made me feel vulnerable. I had a new title. More responsibility. People would ask me questions. I would have to have answers. No looking to my father for guidance. And I was the youngest among my working peers. My age didn't sit well with many businessmen. I would just have to prove to them age didn't matter.

When we got to the hotel, I'd thought Crystal would want to room with me and ditch the room arrangements that had already been made, but she decided she needed her own space. Which was fine. I'd only asked to be a gentleman. Even though we fucked in my plane, twice.

Crystal and I agreed to rest up in our separate hotel rooms and meet up for dinner with our client. A good idea. Had she decided to stay with me, I didn't think resting would be on our agenda.

After what had happened on my plane, things would never be the same between us. Either we stopped before it went further or we moved forward. I didn't know what she thought, but as for me, I wanted to see her again and see how far we could take it.

A knock on my door startled me. Crystal was right on time.

I opened the door. "Good evening."

Her long, skintight black dress had cut my breath short. I might have drooled a bit. The deep vee in the front of her dress showed the curves of her breasts more than I would like them to be seen in a professional meeting. My mind reeled back to the plane, when I was touching and licking those full, round breasts.

"Good evening," Crystal cooed in her seductive voice, the same tone from when she'd first run into me.

Her eyes roamed my frame with approval. My gut told me she had run into me on purpose. Whatever the reason, I didn't care. I was glad she had.

"You look beautiful." I planted a soft kiss between her breasts and then ran my tongue lower. I hadn't planned to do that, but I wanted a taste of my dessert first.

Crystal moaned and shuddered. "You do something like that again, and we're going to be late for dinner. Do you hear me, Mr. Knight?"

"Crystal clear." I winked. A bit cliché, but it made her snort.

"You can do better than that, Mr. CEO. Are you ready? Or are you going to stand around all night?"

I blinked. "Sorry. But you did distract me. So, your fault. I'm ready."

I placed my hand behind her back and guided her to the elevator. After I scanned my key card, the door opened. I used the key card again to take us to the top floor.

"I'm so glad they chose a restaurant in the hotel. So convenient," Crystal said.

"They were accommodating our schedule. I let them know we had to leave tomorrow for Hong Kong."

"Are you ready, Max?" Crystal turned to face the glass, overlooking the city lights. "Amazing. So peaceful."

I stood next to her, gazing at the same view. "Breathtaking, I agree. And yes, I'm ready."

"Just in case, I sent you an email. Items you should bring up during the meeting. Not that you have to take my suggestions." She twisted at the waist and ran a hand down my chest. "You're a big boy. You can handle yourself. Except maybe around me."

Just as the elevator dinged, she slid her hand to the side. I smacked her ass when she stepped out.

She yelped and jerked, then she spun back to me. "You're going to pay for that. I spank back even harder." She gave me a playful glare, promising me a torturous but mind-blowing night.

As soon as we entered, the hostess took us to a private room. With her hair in a tight bun, she wore a traditional Korean dress with a pink skirt, and a pretty flower design on a white background for the top.

"I would love to wear one," Crystal whispered. "Gorgeous."

"I know a place you can get one handmade."

"If we have time. Our schedule is so packed."

We passed down a hallway decorated with traditional Korean fans. Each fan had been hand-painted with a story, but I had no idea what they were about.

The CEO, the president, and vice-president of *Korean Fashion Magazine* stood to greet us when we entered a sleek, modern room.

"Mr. Park. Mr. Kim. Mr. Cho." I addressed them one by one and shook their hands. Afterward I introduced them to Crystal.

All eyes went straight to her cleavage and then to her face. I didn't blame them. I had done the same. However, they gave her the same respect as they had given me and shook her hand.

Crystal surprised me by saying hello in Korean.

The men looked at her as if she had spoken a foreign language they didn't understand at first, and then they all chuckled and smiled, welcoming her American-accented greeting.

"Please, have a seat," Mr. Park said with a slight bow. After he settled into his chair, he closed the menu. "I took the liberty of ordering their finest. I hope you don't mind."

"No, not at all," I said. "Thank you. Besides, I've always depended on gracious hosts like you to guide me."

"I hope you ordered bulgogi and japchae. Those are my favorite dishes."

The men smiled and nodded their heads.

"Yes, we did, Ms. Blackwell. You've had them before?" Mr. Kim asked.

"Why, of course, Mr. Kim. I love Korean food. I believe Korean food is the best of all Asian cuisine."

Clever, Crystal. Stroke his ego.

Mr. Kim nodded, a huge smile plastered on his face. "Your favorite. Very good. I think I like you."

Crystal showed all her gleaming white teeth. "So, have you visited Los Angeles before?"

"No. But we plan to," Mr. Cho answered.

"Good. When you come, we'll have to take you to one of our finest restaurants. It's called McDonald's. Have you heard of it?"

The men let out a full belly laugh.

"She knows how to joke. I like your associate, Mr. Knight." Mr. Park took a sip of his water after his chuckles subsided.

I freakin' love her at the moment.

Crystal knew how to play them. She was the expert fisher, hooking them and reeling them into her hands.

Something went up my leg. Crystal's foot. She had taken one of her heels off. So naughty. But I loved it. She was daring, bold, and she knew what she wanted.

The waitress came to serve us tea, set down small dishes of assorted food, and left.

"Please. Go ahead." Mr. Kim tipped his head.

"I love banchan." Crystal flexed her chopsticks. "I could just eat that and be full. I especially love kimchee."

The men grinned, taking in her beaming eyes.

"Mr. Park," I began, watching Crystal use her chopsticks to pick up some spicy radishes. "Can you share why your company has not taken to our online magazine?"

Mr. Park took a gulp of his beer and tapped at his glass. "Knight Fashion changed overnight. It might not affect your company in America, but sudden changes don't fare well with ours. You have to give us time to adjust."

Crystal froze, her eyes darting with thoughts. "What if we gave them an incentive? Three-month trial for free. Doesn't matter what country you live in, doesn't matter what language you speak, everyone loves free things. Even wealthy people love to receive free things. Don't you agree?"

The men exchanged glances with one another, nodding.

"We certainly could try," Mr. Cho said. "I believe that will help."

"Oh, sorry." Crystal lowered her head. "I'm not in the position to make such decisions, but Mr. Knight can. But if it's okay with him, I can handle the responsibility. After all, I am head of Customer Relations.

I rested my hand on her shoulder. "Great idea. I'll have you lead this project."

"Perfect. Thank you so much." Crystal's hand went higher on my thigh.

"We have other things to discuss, but looks like the food is here." I leaned back in my seat as the waitress brought over the dishes.

"We have all night." Mr. Park raised his glass.

We all did the same.

Chapter 8
Crystal

Time ticked away as we drank, laughed, and talked business. The *Korean Fashion Magazine* agreed to our three-month free trial and also agreed to promote the hell out of it. This would be a huge turn of events for Knight Fashion. If the free trial succeeded, then we could suggest the same in China, Japan, and so on.

Sometimes Max placed a hand on my lap, and sometimes he draped an arm around the back of my chair. Intentionally or by accident, I didn't know. But I loved the feel of his closeness, as if we were a couple.

Max set his cup down. "Well, it's getting late. I don't want to keep you away from your family."

Good one, Max. What a smooth way to say, Let's end the meeting.

"Our wives are used to it." Mr. Cho chuckled, his face as red as the beautiful arrangement of roses on the table behind him.

Mr. Park checked his watch, his neck as flushed as his cheeks from the wine. "But you are right. I don't know about Mr. Kim and Mr. Cho, but I have a meeting early in the morning."

"We Asians look like red apples." Mr. Kim pointed at his friends. "You both, on the other hand, you're lucky you can drink alcohol and not look like you had way too much."

"But your women have beautiful skin and so do you." I leaned closer and smiled.

"Ah, beautiful skin." Mr. Kim patted his face. "Must go home to wife. I already took care of the bill before you came."

"Thank you very much," Max said. "The dinner was outstanding."

"Yes, thank you." I gave a curt nod. "Thank you for a lovely meeting. The food was absolutely delicious, and your company will be unforgettable. You'll have a new contract tomorrow with Mr. Knight's approval. The sooner we get this started, the faster we all make money."

The men laughed and smiled at me, and I laid on the charm thicker. Mr. Park rose, the other two did as well, and Max and I followed suit.

"I like the way Ms. Blackwell thinks," Mr. Park said. "How long are you staying in town?"

"We're leaving tomorrow," Max said.

"That's a short trip, but I understand." Mr. Cho pushed in his chair and came around to shake my hand again.

After we said our farewells, we all headed down together, and they left with their own drivers. Then Max and I made our way back inside.

"Come walk with me?" Max offered his hand. "Unless you're tired?"

"Me tired? I do all-nighters, and sometimes it's not for work." I gave him a playful smirk.

Max lifted an eyebrow and I linked my arm to his. He took me to a restaurant bar in the hotel, and a hostess took us to a private area toward the back. We sat on opposite sides of the booth.

Our waitress giggled and couldn't keep her eyes off Max. For the first time, jealousy tugged at my gut. I had felt the emotion before, but not to this degree. That meant I was getting pulled in. After the waitress took our order, she left.

"Is this a date?" I caressed his hand resting on the table.

His lips tugged at the corners. "A mini one. When we get back, I would love to take you out on a proper date."

"As opposed to … is this a fake date?"

Max chuckled, his laughter infectious and so damn hot.

"Of course not. I want to get to know you. Is that okay?"

"I would like that, and I would love to get to know you too. So what do you want to know about me? Ask away."

Max waited for the waitress to place our drinks down before he said, "Tell me about your family." He took a sip of his coffee.

I tapped on my hot mug filled with green tea. "I have a younger sister. Her name is Candice, she's an attorney, and she lives in Texas with her boyfriend. My parents are not together. I was happy the day they got a divorce. They had a horrible marriage. I can only recall them constantly bickering. And there you have it." I shrugged. "What about you? I know you have a younger brother, but every family has a dirty secret." I snorted.

"Some dirtier than others." Max took another gulp.

"You took your father's position. What about your brother? This is a family business, is it not?"

"My brother has been through some rough times. He should be traveling as we speak. He'll join me when he's ready. I don't want someone who's half here."

"I understand. And your parents? The pictures I see of them in the *LA Times* or fashion magazines, they look so happy."

Max glanced at the people sitting at the bar then focused back to me. "They are. But they had their rough moments. Nobody is perfect. It's how you deal with the situation that will define the relationship. My mom quit her career to help my dad fulfill his dream. My brother and I were raised by two wonderful nannies, but my parents were there for us and for each other. It was tough. But our family is in a great position because of the sacrifice."

"I think I adore you even more." I gave him a soft smile. "I think both of my parents were very selfish. They put their careers first, over each other and my sister and me. Perhaps some people aren't meant to have children or a family. I mean, why bother trying if you're determined to put your career above all?"

"Some people can't help it, I suppose. Once I settle down and have a family, I'm going to hire someone else to do all the traveling."

I circled my finger around the brim of the mug, wondering if I should ask the question. "So, do you expect your wife to be home, raising your children?"

Max stretched his legs and leaned forward. "Not if she doesn't want to. I don't think women have to sacrifice their career to have a family. It's all workable. Give and take. What do you think?"

Trick question?

I scratched an itch by my ear and sighed. "I wasn't born into a wealthy home, so I had to make ends meet on my own. I've had a job since I was a senior in high school, and I've worked all my life since then. Even when I went to college, I had to work. It was tough, but I did it."

"I admire you for that. I had everything paid for, handed to me on a silver platter."

I smiled, and his compliment made me blush. "Anyway, I think I would need to work for security. I never want to rely on anyone financially, no matter how rich my husband is."

"Good point." Max took another drink and placed his empty mug to the side of the table.

"Would you like another tea?" I asked.

"No. Thank you. If I drink any more, I'm going to pee all night."

Max's chest rose and fell with a chuckle. He looked so good with the dim light casting over him, highlighting his hair, his eyes, those high cheekbones, and those lips I wanted to ravish.

A comfortable silence fell, and I listened to the instrumental music playing softly in the background.

"What are you looking for, Crystal? What are your hopes and dreams?"

Someone like you.

"I've dated enough guys to tell the difference between the jerks and the good ones."

Max hiked an eyebrow. "Have you had a long-term relationship before? I'm going to assume you're not in one at the moment."

I frowned and glanced up the high ceiling and back to him. "I dated someone for two years. That was my longest, but obviously it didn't work out. He wasn't supportive of my career decisions. He wanted me at his beck and call every day after work and on the weekend. We fought every time I went out with my friends. He either had insecurity issues or he didn't trust me. What about you? You've got quite the reputation."

Max scrubbed his face and released the tight tension on his features. "The problem with the media, they make us guys ..." He pointed to his chest. "the villains. I've dated many women. I'm not going to lie about that, but I told them from the beginning that I wasn't looking for a serious relationship. A handful of them were. I suppose they hoped I would change my mind, so when I was snapped taking someone else to lunch or dinner, it was all over the news that I was the cheating type. People need to get their story straight before they publish something that could ruin someone's reputation."

I waved a hand. "Don't worry. Most people don't believe the bullshit anyway. So, no one special for you either, then? No one you're crying over or hoping to get back together with? You know, I gotta be sure."

"No. No one."

"Good … I think." I lowered my gaze. I probably shouldn't have said those words. To remedy what I couldn't take back, I said, "Anyway, it's best we get some sleep."

Max rose and waited for me. "We have an early flight, though the plane won't take off without me."

I snickered. "True. So very true."

After he walked me to my room, he went to his. I'd thought about knocking at his door and seducing him. But I was too tired.

Max was an upstanding man, the kind you don't let go. I had to make him mine.

Chapter 9
Maxwell

We fucked in the plane on the way home. But now that we were back to reality, I needed her to think about what she wanted from me.

Working together and dating was not the ideal situation, but you can't help who you fall in love with. I wouldn't say I loved her already, but I was fascinated with her mind, not to mention her work ethic. The week of working together really showed me how she was excellent at her position. Flirting was a bonus.

I'd planned to spend Saturday recovering from the time change and catching up at work, but a friend from college texted that he'd be in town only this weekend. So I met him for lunch in Hollywood.

"How's your brother?" Jason asked after we ordered our meal.

"He's doing better. He visited us and he looked good. I'm sure he has bad days, but he's trying. I wish I could help him."

He took a sip of his water. "Traveling alone can be soul searching. I understand you want to help him. If that happened to my brother, I would feel the same.

But you can only be there for him. He'll have to get over it in his own time. What happened to him is messed up."

I sighed.

"So, anyone special?" Jason slowly spread his lips. "Uh … there is. I can tell by the idiot smile on your face."

I leaned back into my seat. "I'm smiling at you. I'm happy to see you after so long. Your fault for moving to New York."

He shrugged. "Gotta go where the job is. Unless you want to pay me."

"I could find you a position. I mean it."

"Thanks, but no thanks. You going to hire a full-time doctor?" He chuckled. "Anyway, long distance is good for us. That way you'll miss me. So tell me about this girl."

"Nothing to tell yet."

He regarded me for a moment and leaned back. "Bullshit. You slept with her."

I frowned. "How the hell can you tell by looking at me?"

His green eyes gleamed. "I can't. I thought I'd just say it and see if you'd admit it. And you did."

"Asshole." I chuckled.

"You're the only person who calls me that, but I guess I deserve it. So, is she the one? I've been waiting for you to settle down so we can take trips together."

I waited for the waitress to set our drinks on the table and leave. "I like her, a lot."

"Then why the hesitation?"

"She's my employee. From what I've seen so far in such a short amount of time, she's good at her job. If things go wrong, I lose a great customer relations director."

"But what if things go right? You'll have both."

I planted my elbows on the table and ran a hand across my face. "You always look at the positive side of things."

"That's what I'm here for. To be a pain in your ass." He cackled.

I raised my glass. "To you and Julie for being the biggest pains in my ass."

He raised his glass to mine. "To the possibilities. Take them or lose them."

While we ate, Crystal texted me.

Crystal: *Hello, Max. Do you have plans for dinner?*

Max: *No. What did you have in mind?*

Crystal: *You and me, dinner and then dessert? I'll bring both.*

Max: *I like the sound of that. What kind of dessert?*

Crystal: *It's called chocolate Crystal cake.*

Max: *Sounds delicious.*

Crystal: *You'll never want another dessert after you have a taste.*

Max: *I can't wait.*

It was time to figure out what I wanted and to put my wants into action.

I tried to hide my smile from Jason but failed. He laughed at me and shook his head with a grin.

Chapter 10
Crystal

I took a chance texting Max. For all I knew, he had plans. Perhaps even a date. But he text back fairly quickly, and we even flirted.

I took a deep breath and knocked on the front door of his penthouse. Of course he would live in such a luxurious place.

Max opened the door and spread his lips wide. He had such a good-looking smile. His whole face lit up just for me, and I took in the look I pretended he only gave to me.

"Hello, Max." I handed him a large carrier filled with chicken pasta, salad, and dinner rolls. "Next time you can come over to my place, and I'll even cook for you. Unfortunately, this is takeout."

"Thank you for the offer, and thank you for going out of your way."

While Max took the bag to the kitchen, I went to the window that took up the whole back wall, showing the dazzling city lights.

"You have an amazing view," I said. "It reminds me of New York." I swung around to see Max right in front of me.

His attire made him look playful and young. His jeans hugged him and a loose, button-up long-sleeve shirt went well with the casual look he was going for. But his hungry, predatory gaze made me hot all over.

"You promised me dessert, Crystal. I usually have my dessert first. Where's my chocolate Crystal cake you offered?" he asked with a soft but demanding voice, the kind that thrilled me, left me almost powerless.

I flicked my hair to one side and unbuttoned my trench coat to reveal black, lacy lingerie. "If you want it, come and get it."

His eyes raked over me and stripped me bare, and then he conquered me with his lips and arms. Then Max guided me to the spare room and gently laid me on the bed.

"You enjoy teasing me?" He ripped the top of the lingerie, exposing my breast. First the cool air and then Max's hot breath so close to my nipple nearly had me undone.

I moaned, arching my back. "I love the way you respond to me." I gripped his hair and pulled him to me. "I love fucking you. I think about it all the time."

As he sucked my nipple, his finger went inside me, slipping into my wetness and dragging out over my clit. Again. And again.

"You make me feel so good, Max. I want more of you." I panted between each word. My body exploded with pleasure, wanting him inside me.

"This is just the beginning," he said, pulling back to take his clothes off.

Max hovered over me, his hand roaming over my body, from my breasts and then lower. He took his time kissing and discovering every inch of my body.

I wanted to give him the same pleasure he had given me, so I pushed him back on the mattress and leaned over him.

"My turn."

I crawled up like a lioness stalking her prey. When I was at the perfect spot, I licked his dick from base to tip.

Max moaned and his hips thrust upward.

I sucked him into my mouth and worked him harder and faster, pumping the length of his shaft with my hand. He was so beautiful. Every muscle of him tensed.

"Come here." Max pulled me to him.

"Did I do something wrong?"

"No." He caressed my hair. "You give a damn good blow job. But I don't want to come. We've got all night."

We've got all night. He wanted me to stay?

"Then what are you waiting for, Mr. Knight?"

He growled. His fingers slipped through my hair and pulled me in for a fervent kiss, as if he couldn't get enough. As he released me, his teeth grazed my lips.

I gasped when he twisted our bodies and I ended up on my back. Then he dragged me to the edge of the bed and stepped off.

"I'm going to fuck you until you scream my name."

Oh. My. God. Take me now, Max.
And he did.
He fucked me until hours passed, until I was dead tired.
We lay there side by side, the heat of his body touching mine. I rested my head in the crook of his neck with our fingers intertwined by his chest.
"You're amazing." He kissed the back of my hand.
"So are you." I ran a hand across his chest.
"I think that was the best dessert I've ever had." He brushed my lips ever so lightly.
"Told you." I shrugged.
Max chuckled. "You must be starving."
"Famished."
"I'll go heat up dinner." He tapped my nose. "But you take your time and rest up. After dinner, you're mine."
I didn't know what came over me, but while he was in the kitchen heating up our dinner without clothes on, I walked toward him naked with my high heels on. Max lifted me on the counter and took me again.
After dinner, we went to the room and used my torn lingerie to tie his hands. I wanted him to beg, and so he did.
"I have to be honest. I believe three orgasms is the most I've had in one day." I snuggled in his arms. "You know, most men ask how many partners I've been with, but you never did. Why?"

Max caressed my face, lifted a strand of hair around my ear. "It's none of my business. You already told me about your long-term relationship. The number doesn't matter. You're a high-class woman who wouldn't sleep with just any man. In fact, I think you choose wisely."

"You're amazing, you know that?" I ran a hand down his bicep, feeling its curve and the hardness.

"I've been told that." He snorted.

"So where do we go from here? Are we just fuck buddies?"

Max chuckled. "Now that's a first. If that's all you want, then I'll have no choice but to agree."

"And if I want more? More as in dating, getting to know you better, and maybe having a future kind of deal?"

"I would like that too."

I beamed a smile and cuddled closer, melding my body to his. I'd never felt so loved and wanted. I wanted Max, all of him. I didn't want just the dating. Eventually I would want to be his wife.

"Then dating it is," I said. "So does this mean exclusive or not? I just want to clarify, because I have a long list of men waiting to call me."

Max poked my breast, not hard, but to startle me. "You can burn your list. No one gets to touch what's mine. When I date, I'm exclusive. I don't believe in sharing."

Music to my ears. The words I wanted to hear.

"Are we crystal clear? I had to say it." Max laughed, the full belly kind.

"No more crystal jokes." I poked him again and again until Max lifted himself over me.

He grabbed the fabric I used to tie him up and waved it at me. The dark gleam in his eyes told me what he planned to do with the fabric.

My body trembled. I was already wet for him.

Chapter 11
Maxwell

I sent Crystal a bouquet of red roses to her house to thank her for bringing dinner and for an amazing night. I also sent her flowers a week after that to celebrate our one week. Kind of cheesy, one might think, but I had a feeling she might appreciate the sentiment.

A month later, Crystal had been coming over just about every night. I even gave her a set of keys to my place. I wanted to proceed at a slow pace, but somehow Crystal managed to weasel her way to more.

Before I knew it, she had practically moved in. But what the hell. Life was short. Might as well make the most of it.

We hadn't disclosed our relationship to our co-workers. In fact, we hid it well, even when Crystal visited me often in my office during lunch hours. We played it off as having a lunch business meeting.

Mandy called on the intercom. "Mr. Knight. Ms. Blackwell is here to see you."

The door buzzed and Crystal walked in and closed it behind her.

"You wanted to see me, Mr. Knight?"

Crystal wore a tight knit sweater dress that clung to her body. She also wore her hair down.

"Have a seat," I said. "I wanted your opinion on the color scheme. We had a meeting regarding this matter."

Crystal sat and glanced over me at the table. "You ordered lunch?"

"I took the liberty of catering lunch for us. I hope you don't mind. It's Chinese."

"I love Chinese food. I know a great Chinese restaurant nearby."

"By any chance, is it called Szechuan Palace?" I asked.

Her eyes beamed. "Yes. We have the same great taste."

"I believe food is not the only thing we have in common, don't you agree?"

She gave me a wicked glance. "I *so* agree."

"Shall we get lunch?" I tilted my head behind me. Crystal rose. "I would love to."

"Buffet style for two."

"Why not? It's the best kind." She smiled.

Just then the clouds opened up and the sun peeked through, highlighting her hair to almost white, and the blue in her eyes looked silver.

"You have a beautiful view," she said, serving herself some Kung Pao chicken.

"I do." I looked straight at her.

Her cheeks turned slightly pink. After she scooped some fried rice and assorted vegetables, she walked to the sofa. I followed and sat next to her.

"I'll be heading to New York Fashion Week in a couple of weeks." I used the chopsticks to pick up some chicken and shoved it in my mouth.

Crystal crossed her legs and studied me. "Is this an invitation, or are you letting me know your agenda? Because it's not on my calendar."

I went back to the table and picked up two bottles of water. "It's not on your calendar, and no, this is not an invitation."

Crystal stiffened. She even stopped chewing. "Oh. Glad you made that clear."

Her tone hinted at sarcasm, but she remained professional.

"It's not that I don't want you to come with me. We can't always travel together for work, but we can for personal reasons."

She swallowed and used her chopsticks to pick up a piece of broccoli into her mouth. "Yes. I know. That's why I asked." She flashed a quick smile.

"Good. I'm glad you understand. To tell you the truth, a part of me worried."

Crystal snorted. "Oh, please, Max. We're professionals. I know there'll be times when you'll have to do your own thing. Though I would love to accompany you to New York Fashion Week another time. I've never been."

"I'll make it happen, but sorry, not this time. I need you to take care of the Asian market. I also need you to make some phone calls. The Japanese are sending their rep to visit us."

"During Fashion Week? Don't they attend?"

"Yes, but again, they're sending their reps at the same time."

Crystal took a drink from her water bottle and placed it down. "I see. So in two weeks? Will you be gone the whole week?"

I bit down on my snow pea. "Yes, and a few days more. I'm going to visit a friend."

"Oh. A friend." Her tone elevated, and she looked away.

That was the first time I got a taste of the unexpected jealous side of her.

"My friend Jason. We're college friends. He and his wife live in New York."

She smiled. "You should visit your friend. I'm sure it's difficult being so far away."

I dipped my eyes lower to my almost empty plate. "I do wish we lived closer. Anyway, I've never heard you speak of your friends."

She twisted in her seat to face me. "I have none. Women all hate me."

Her tone was so serious I almost believed her until she chuckled.

"Oh, Max. I'm just kidding. I have friends, but they're scattered throughout the states. I have a few close high school friends nearby, but they're busy. A couple of them have children."

"Do I get to meet them?" I placed my plate on the table and leaned back into the sofa.

"Only if I get to meet yours too." She gave me a smirk.

Crystal leaned back and spread her legs, one over the back of the sofa.

"Is this an invitation?" I stroked the length of her leg.

"Yes, it is. I kinda forgot to wear underwear this morning."

I sucked in a breath and ran my hand lower and lower until my thumb landed on her clit. After I circled it a few times, I took my hand away.

"Ms. Blackwell. If you want more, you're going to have to show me. How badly do you want me?" I looked at my watch pretentiously to hint that I could be elsewhere, just to tease her.

I would never make my woman feel like she wasn't worth my time, but Crystal liked a little challenge. And I loved teasing her.

She angled her eyebrows. "I wanted you the second you bumped into me. No, I take that back. I wanted you the moment I laid eyes on you on paper. I read an article about you in *Knight Fashion* magazine, your struggles, your dreams, and all about you. You are the epitome of the perfect man, Maxwell Knight. And I'm so happy that I'm here with you."

I had been with many women. Most of them wanted to date me for my status, fame, and money. Some even wanted to fuck in hopes of getting modeling careers or a job at Knight Fashion.

It was hard to distinguish who wanted me for myself. Her honest words had me speechless. I hadn't given her my heart fully because of my past experiences, but perhaps she could be the one. The one I could trust to be my best friend. My soul mate. My lunch buddy, my something real.

I supposed time would tell. One day at a time. After all, to make any relationship last, there had to be work, give and take, bad and good times. I truly believed any couple who could weather the storm was meant for each other. Perhaps Crystal would be my something real. Too soon to tell, but we seemed to be on the right path so far.

I offered her my hand, and she took it.

"Are we going somewhere?" she asked, her eyes gleaming with curiosity.

"It's time for dessert." I winked. "I'm going to take you on my desk. Don't worry. My office is soundproof."

She twisted her lips. "Good. Because you'll be screaming my name from the things I'm going to do to you."

I smacked her ass. She yelped and jerked forward.

"Is this a challenge?" I asked, planting her on my desk and spreading her legs apart.

She yanked my tie until my face met hers. "It is. You know me so well."

"I do. But sorry, my love, I think we're both going to win this challenge."

After I laid her down, I sucked her clit and made her scream my name.

Continue Max's story-Something Great-a full novel.
Read a sample of:
      Something Great
      When the Wind Chimes
      Once Upon A Legend

Something Great from Jenna's point of view.

The mirrored wall distracted me when my necklace sparkled brilliantly in the reflection. From the corner of my eyes, I saw a figure moving but dismissed it and turned to the elusive restroom sign. I was just about to head in that direction when someone behind me spoke in a deep, manly voice, sending shivers down my back.

"I'm your prescription. Let me be your new addiction." His words glided like butter, smooth and cool.

Startled, I twitched and turned toward his voice. There he was, all six feet of him, peering down at me with a smile that could make me do just about anything. Though there was nothing to laugh about, especially seeing this hottie in front of me, I couldn't help but laugh at the lame pickup line.

He wore beige casual pants and a black sweater fitted perfectly to his toned body. His hair was brushed to the side, showing a nice forehead. Whatever kind of cologne he had on made me want to dive right into his arms, or maybe it wasn't the cologne, but just him.

"Pretty cheesy, huh?" He chuckled.

I shyly smiled as I stared down at my shoes. *What's wrong with me? Answer him.* "Yeah, kind of." I peered up, only to have him take my breath away again.

"Sorry. I just had to say that. You appeared so lost and vulnerable. Do you need some help?"

Great. He looked at me and saw a lost puppy. "I actually found what I was looking for." I stared into his eyes, melting into him.

Snap out of it.

"You certainly did," he said with a playful tone.

Arching my brows in confusion, I mulled over what I'd said. From his perspective, my words had been about him.

"We meet again, for the third time," he said.

He's counting?

He gave me a sidelong glance. "You left so abruptly, I didn't get to ask your name."

My hand went to my chest to hold in my heart thumping too fast. "Oh, my name is Jeanella Mefferd, but you can call me Jenna."

Extending his hand, he waited for mine. "I'm Maxwell. But you can call me Max."

Nervously, I placed my hand in his. He clasped my hand, strong yet gentle, just right, and heat blazed through me from his touch.

"Are you here with someone?"

"Yes." I looked away.

"Are you lost? Do you need some help?"

"Actually, I was looking for the restroom." I slowly pulled my hand back to point in the direction to the hallway. I had just realized he held my hand the whole time during our short conversation. "So, I'd better go."

"I'll walk you there."

What? "Oh, no need. I'm sure I won't get lost."

My face heated up again so I turned before Max could say another word, but he placed his hand gently on my back, guiding me to the ladies' room. I turned my back to the bathroom door to thank him, but he spoke first.

"I think this is my stop," Max murmured, his smoldering eyes meeting mine. "I'm not wanted in there. What do you think?" He arched his brows and his tone held a note of challenge.

Huh? He wants to go in with me?

I gasped silently, still lost in his eyes. "I think the women in there would throw themselves at you."

I couldn't believe I'd said those words. I couldn't take them back. What was I doing flirting with him?

Max's eyes gleamed as he leaned forward. His arms reached out, his muscles flexing as he placed one on each side of me on the wall. With nowhere to go, I was trapped inside the circle of his arms.

Max leaned down toward the left side of my face and brushed my hair with his cheek. "You smell delicious," he whispered.

His hot breath shot tingles to places I hadn't expected.

Out of nervousness and habit, my left index finger flew to my mouth. Max gave a crooked, naughty grin and slowly took my hand.

"Did you know, biting one's finger is an indication one is sexually deprived?" His words came out slowly, playfully. "I can fix that for you, if you'd like."

He did not just say that to me.

I parted my lips for a good comeback, but came up short. My chest rose and fell quickly and I tried to control the desire burning through me. Sure, he'd helped me once, but that didn't mean we were friends, or flirting buddies, or I would allow him to fix my sexual deprivation.

Oh God. Can guys tell if you haven't done it in a considerably long time? This had to stop or else—oh dear—I wanted to take him with me into the restroom.

Needing to put a stop to the heat, I placed my hand on his chest—big mistake. Touching him made it worse, sending electrifying tingles through every inch of me.

He pulled back at my touch, but his eyes did the talking instead. There was no need for words. I felt his hard stare on my body, as if he undressed me with his gorgeous eyes. His eyes caressed me, as real as if they were his hands. I felt them all over my skin, unraveling me.

When I thought I was going to faint, his eyes shifted to mine again.

"It was nice to meet you, Jenna. I'm sure we'll see each other again real soon. I better let you go. Your someone must be waiting for you. By the way ..." He paused as he charmed me with his smile again. "You took my breath away. If I were your someone, I wouldn't let you out of my sight for even a second, because someone like me would surely try to whisk you away." He winked and left.

A sample from **When the Wind Chimes**

"Taxi!" I waved frantically, splashing through the puddles, as I made a mad dash toward it, lowering my head against the pouring rain. The likelihood of snatching the taxi was slim. But I had to try.

A few cars honked as I dodged past. *Not a good idea.* "Sorry," I bellowed, but a roll of thunder drowned out my voice.

The wind had kicked up and practically pushed me across the road. With my bags trying to take flight, I felt like Mary Poppins, only less graceful and more drenched to the bone.

Not a good idea? More like horrible, dangerous, idiotic idea. I could have been hit by a distracted driver. Or I could have slipped, and in the rain, no one would spot me until I'd been flattened. What was I thinking?

But I made it safely across.

I jerked open the door and threw my bags — and my soggy self — into the back.

"Hi." I flipped my damp hair to the side and checked that I'd closed the door. My cold wet clothes stuck to me like a second skin, I sighed with relief and positioned the smaller bag on my lap. "Poipu, please."

Beside me, someone cleared his throat.

I gasped and jerked, my heart thundering with the storm. I hadn't expected anyone else in the backseat, especially a good-looking man with slicked-back dark hair and wide, annoyed eyes.

He smoothed the lapel of his out of place, but classy, gray tailored suit. Who flew to Kauai in business attire? He sure smelled nice, though. A scent of cedar and pine permeated the small space.

Either I was hallucinating my dream guy, or he had gotten in the cab at the same time. But I had been the only crazy person running across traffic. I'd done a quick check before I got in, but the tinted window had prevented me from getting a clear view.

He clutched a dry, folded umbrella on his lap. I waited in case he was a passenger that hadn't gotten out yet. A guy in a suit like that might be hesitant to run into the rain.

He blinked the most beautiful chestnut-colored eyes framed with thick eyebrows. The intensity of his stare drew me in and made me forget about the pelting rain, but I imagined cozy nights and intimate dinners. Then a muscle twitched in his jaw, and he wiped away the water I had flicked on his face with my hair.

I covered my mouth in horror. *Oops.*

"I'm … I'm so sorry." I swallowed, expecting him to yell or shoo me out of the cab. "I didn't see you. I'll just go." But I didn't move.

It'd take forever to get another taxi, because I'd have to get back in the long line and wait my turn. When I finally broke the gaze, I clamped my fingers around the metal door handle just as a gentle hand rested on my shoulder.

"It's fine. You stay. I was just leaving."

Combined with the tension in the car, his swoony eyes, and the unexpected touch, his smooth baritone sent a surge of pleasant electricity through me. It had been so long since I'd felt this magnitude of attraction ...

Forget it!

He was probably leaving for a business trip, anyway—he was dressed much better than the average tourist. But then the taxi would have dropped him off at the departure terminal and not across the street.

"What do you mean?" The driver twisted at his waist and propped an arm along the seat back. "You just got in. I can take you both."

The man gave an uncomfortable laugh. In spot-on timing with the song "Baby It's Cold Outside," playing softly in the background, the man said, "I can't stay."

Keep me company. I parted my mouth and the words almost escaped. I was surprised how much I hoped he would. So much for my holiday vow to forget men.

"It's okay. You can stay. I mean, you do what you want. I'm sorry I got you ..." I winced. "Wet. I honestly didn't see you there. We can share a cab, and I am more than willing to pay."

Stop rambling.

"No need to apologize," he said in that smooth voice.

"But —"

Before I could say more, he stepped out and raised his black umbrella, shielding himself as he leaned over the door.

"Brandon, take this lovely lady where she needs to go. Put it on my tab and add the same amount of tip as usual."

"Thanks, Lee."

Did he just call me lovely?

"What? Wait."

"Have a good day. Don't worry about me. I can call my driver." He offered a gorgeous crooked grin and shut the door.

I twisted around to get a better look at him and watched him strut away like the weather was perfect. Like a dream, he faded into the pouring rain.

Continue on this link:
https://amzn.to/3DPOmCa

A sample from Once Upon A Legend

The Mausoleum

Merrick

Icy fingers of grief gripped my heart as I ran across
I the courtyard bricks with a stargazer lily in my hand.
Crisp dawn air filled my lungs. Despite the biting wind,
sweat dampened my forehead and heat surged under my
skin. Chest heaving, I slowed onto the road that led to the
royal family mausoleum, about a mile from the castle.

The circular tomb towered over the broad plain.
Twelve massive pillars carved from the same gray stone
held up the domed ceiling. Above the entrance a symbol,
the Eternal Ring, had been etched. Six concentric rings, like
ripples from a stone dropped in water, representing the six
aspects of magic: soil, air, fire, water, light, and dark.

The sentinels painted on the outer wall held out their
swords, protecting the royal dead. I stopped to read the
adage from our ancestors etched along the archway of the
iron door: *Death is only the beginning of our path to what
is beyond. Enter with clarity. Enter with love. Enter to
celebrate new life.*

I focused on the keyhole and curled my index finger, allowing a kernel of magic to flow through me with a warm, tingling sensation. The metal door creaked as it swung open. I took the first step down and swiped at cobwebs. The scrape of iron meeting stone echoed inside when the door locked behind me.

I stilled as a cold breeze stroked my face like a soft wave of ocean mist, and musty air tickled my nose. Swallowed up by walls built by long gone ancestors, I quickened my breath.

Breathe, Merrick. There are no ghosts in here. Don't be a coward.

Dust particles danced like butterflies within a shaft of light. The glass dome overhead not only let in the morning sun, but illuminated the painting of three stunning goddesses—Mothers Nimue, Viviane, and Myneve—on the glass, casting jewel-toned prisms over the caskets. Their hands interlocked on the hilt, the blade blazing a white fire. The Eternal Mothers' flowing dresses and their long silver hair glowed like moonstone against the light.

All former rulers of the Dumonian Empire and their descendants had been buried here. The most recent casket, my mother's, lay on a raised dais, circled by twelve steps. It had been months since illness had taken her life, but it seemed like only the day before.

I prepared my heart to be crushed again as I climbed the last steps.

"Your favorite, Mother." I swallowed hard and placed a pink stargazer lily on top of the glass casket over the spot where her hands crossed on her chest. I'd plucked one from the castle garden on my way every time I visited her.

Mother's face was almost alive. Her closed eyes were coated with teal, her cheeks with rose, and her lips ruby. Small, hammered-gold leaves intertwined with white baby's breath crowned her forehead and wove through her brunette hair.

She wore a long, alabaster dress, and she looked like a goddess in deep slumber. Regardless of how peaceful she appeared, my heart knotted with gut-wrenching pain.

Through Father's magic, Mother's body had been preserved. She would stay beautiful forever and so would the white rose petals scattered inside the casket.

"Mother, I'm here. You look like you're sleeping." As my words caught in my throat, I brushed my fingertip over the medallion Mother had given me before she passed away.

***

Mother almost knocked the water bowl by her bed when she fished something out under her pillow with a trembling hand. "My gift to you. You will need it one day."

Her fever never relented, even after all the medicine she had taken. The healer couldn't diagnose her disease or its cause. He'd only said that her illness could be a remnant of the Blood Plague that had killed so many infants the year I was born.

Mother uncurled her fingers, revealing a thin leather braid looped through a six-ringed silver pendant.

"An Eternal Ring?" I cradled the medallion with both hands. The polished metal, cold and smooth to touch, seemed ordinary, but Mother wouldn't have given it to me if it weren't special.

"This necklace was passed down within my family. I received it from my mother when she ..." Her weary voice stumbled on the final word. "Passed."

"Nonsense, Mother. You will get better. We just have to calm the fever." My weak voice faltered in its effort to give her hope as I tied the leather around my neck.

"No." Mother spoke with more energy than a sick woman should have. "Listen carefully." She pulled me closer until my ear rested on her fever-scorched lips. "The walls have eyes and ears. Be careful what you say. Trust no one, especially your father. Not even your brothers. One of your brothers will betray you. I've seen it in dreams. I have a gift of foretelling. No one knows, not even your father."

I jerked away, bristling at the seeds of distrust she planted. Father, Rodern, and Jediah, the only family I would have after Mother passed. If I couldn't trust my own family, who could I trust?

Mother was near death and delirious. She had been talking rubbish ever since she became ill, so I played along to give her peace.

"If your heart is worthy and pure, this pendant will help you in dark times," she said.

I wiped beaded sweat from her forehead with a cloth and placed it back inside a water bowl. "How will it help me?"

"That will depend on you. It works differently for everyone."

I rubbed a thumb over the ridges of the six rings. In all the years we'd been taught magic, Mother had never once mentioned a pendant. It looked ordinary, though she claimed it wasn't. But how could I trust what she'd told me in her delirious state of mind?

What was so significant about it?

"Thank you, Mother. I'll treasure it forever." I shuddered a quiet breath, trying to remain strong, as her chest rose and fell with much effort. But her gentle smile said she was pleased.

Mother sensed my torment and rested her blazing fingers over my wrist. "It's okay, Son. It's what the goddesses wanted of me. Do not weep for me when I'm gone. I will be silently walking beside you, and I will always watch over you. I love you, Merrick. Even when I'm gone, I'll love you still."

Her whispered words slammed into my chest, crushing my lungs to leave me breathless. I dropped my head on the mattress and stripped away the man I'd become, down to the small boy for the last time, and let the tears fall.

***

I opened my eyes as my head rested against the cold, unforgiving glass of my mother's casket. Rolling back my shoulders, I shoved away the memory.

Trust no one, especially your father. One of your brothers will betray you. I had become a prisoner of those words, always looking behind me.

After I gave Mother a reverent bow, I dashed down the stairs. Morning meal awaited, and Father would be expecting me.

I pushed the door open with a wave of my hand and sprinted out. Then I peered over my shoulder to ensure the door closed. As I admired the ruby-red glow stretching across the endless blue sky, I ran with Mother's love.

I knew her spirit watched over me. If she could talk, she would say … *Run, Merrick. Do not be late. Trust no one.*

About the Author

Born in Seoul, Korea, author Mary Ting is an international bestselling, multi-gold award winning author. Her books span a wide range of genres, and her storytelling talents have earned a devoted legion of fans, as well as garnered critical praise. She is a diverse voice who writes diverse characters, often dealing with a catastrophic world.

Becoming an author happened by chance. It was a way to grieve the death of her beloved grandmother and inspired by a dream she had in high school. After realizing she wanted to become a full-time author, Mary retired from teaching. She also had the privilege of touring with the Magic Johnson Foundation to promote literacy and her children's chapter book: No Bullies Allowed.

www.authormaryting.com
Bookbub: https://www.bookbub.com/profile/mary-ting
News Update: http://www.tangledtalesofting.com/subscribe/
Group page: https://bit.ly/3tyVy0q

SOMETHING REAL

Facebook: https://www.facebook.com/AuthorMaryTing
Instagram: http://instagram.com/authormaryting
Twitter: @MaryTing https://twitter.com/MaryTing
Website: http://www.tangledtalesofting.com
Email: authormaryting@outlook.com

Made in the USA
Middletown, DE
02 February 2023

23751145R00044